ADJUSTABLE JULIE

JOYCE WILLIAMS

ADJUSTABLE
JULIE

Pictures by HAZEL HOECKER

1137

BROADMAN PRESS • Nashville, Tennessee

Suggested Classification: JF
Library of Congress Catalog Card Number: 76-113214
Printed in the United States of America
15.O6918

Contents

1

A New Home

"Julie! I need you to adjust the blinds, please!" called Mrs. Grey from the living room. There was no answer.

Julie Grey sat on the front steps of her new home. Her head rested against the bricks. The sunshine felt warm. It made her a wee bit sleepy!

From the top of her high stool, Mrs. Grey looked down at the floor. Then she called again. "The sun is shining right in my eyes—please hurry, Julie."

Sadly, Julie moved from her warm spot on the front steps. She dragged her feet as she crossed the porch. Slowly she opened the door, reached inside, and pulled the venetian blind cord.

"Thanks! It's great to see again," sang out Mrs. Grey. "We'll have this place looking like home in no time. Can you help a bit?" she asked, hopefully.

"Why don't we wait for Daddy to hang the drapes?" came Julie's sullen reply.

"Oh, I've hung lots of drapes, Julie," explained Mother. "A house is a home once the furniture is in place and the drapes are hung."

Julie's thoughts closed out her mother's voice. She tiptoed quietly back to her spot on the front steps. Inside, Mother was still talking. She heard the words—new school—new church—friends—Woodridge.

"Why—why—why?" wondered Julie. "Why was HER family always the one to move? Why did Daddy have to stay behind? Why did she and Mother and Tabby have to come HERE?"

Tabby! "Where was that cat?" thought Julie, as she jumped up to search. "I'm sure she doesn't like to move any better than I do!"

The unhappy little girl made good time getting from the front porch steps to the sunlighted patio.

She stopped suddenly!

How disgusting!

There lay Tabby curled into an orange ball on the seat of the lounge chair. She was content as could be, asleep in the sunshine!

Julie's shoulders began to shake. "Just because," she moaned, "just because you have your old cushion to sleep on—you are happy!" Sobs came from deep inside her body. "What if you had to leave important things behind?" She threw herself on the lounge chair beside Tabby.

2

A New School

"I notice from Julie's records that you have moved a number of times," said Mr. Peterson, principal of Woodridge School.

"Yes, we have, Mr. Peterson, but I'm sure Julie will adjust," replied Mrs. Grey.

There was that word again—ADJUST! Adjust the blinds, Julie! Adjust the heat, Julie! Tabby will adjust, Julie!

"ADJUST," thought Julie, "must be Mother's favorite word." She held the strap on her purse so tightly it began to cut into her hand.

"Mrs. Grey, we are glad you sent Julie's records to us. It has given us a chance to place her—Room 27," said Mr. Peterson. "Mrs. King is one of our best teachers. The children love her," he added.

"Room 27—wonder where that is?" thought Julie. She walked slower and slower behind Mother and Mr. Peterson. They had not noticed that she lagged behind. Down a long hall—up some stairs—down another hall. Mother and Mr. Peterson had stopped.

"Julie," Mr. Peterson announced when she finally caught up, "the boys and girls are on the playground, but Mrs. King is here. Let's meet her!"

Julie kept her eyes on the floor. She drew the blocks in the tile with the toe of her shoe. Then she saw a shadow in the doorway. Not a very big shadow, but Julie wanted to run. With Mother's hand on her shoulder that would not be easy. Mother turned Julie toward Room 27. A small woman with big, black eyes stood in the doorway.

"Hi, Julie," said Mrs. King in a friendly voice. "I knew you were coming. We have your desk all ready. Your books and supplies are inside. Do you have money for lunch in your purse?"

The voice sounded nice. The eyes looked nice. For a minute Julie almost forgot her plan to play deaf and dumb. She opened her mouth to speak. Just then a line of boys and girls stopped by the door of Room 27.

12

3

Room 27

The desk in the front row was just right for Julie.
Inside she could feel her books. Mrs. King walked to
the front board. In big letters she wrote FRIEND.

Julie sat very still. She hoped the tears were not going
to spill out. She didn't want friends! All she wanted
right now was to get out of this room and hide.

"Would any boy or girl like to tell me what we decided about this word?" asked Mrs. King. A tall, skinny
boy raised his hand.

"Yes, Frank?" said Mrs. King.

"Well, in Room 27 we are all learning to be friends," answered Frank.

"Right. Anything else?" she asked. The girl in the seat next to Julie raised her hand. Mrs. King nodded to her.

"Someone said that if we want a friend, we have to be one," she said politely.

"Good, Dana, do you think it works?" asked Mrs. King.

"Sure does!" answered Dana, smiling happily.

"Our new friend," announced Mrs. King, turning to the board to print, "is JULIE GREY. We are glad she has come. Now when we play games we'll have even teams again—fourteen on each side."

Julie watched Mrs. King! How little she was! And how pretty. Not at all like her last teacher. What was it Mr. Peterson said—The children love her. Well, the children didn't love Mrs. Stone. It was just luck that she never found out they called her "stoneface." Wonder when Mrs. King is going to stop smiling and begin to yell.

"Who remembers the other important thing we decided about friends?" continued Mrs. King.

A cute little girl, whose brown eyes twinkled and long braids swished from side to side, raised her hand.

"I know that—it is about practicing. We decided that to do anything well we have to practice—even being good friends," said Janice.

"That's great," beamed Mrs. King, "we don't want to forget that one!" Again she turned to the board to write.

1. WE CAN ALL BE FRIENDS.
2. IF YOU WANT A FRIEND, BE ONE.
3. TO DO THINGS WELL, WE MUST PRACTICE.

Mrs. King faced the class. "The paper monitors may pass the drawing paper," she directed. "Each of you may write one of the rules about friends on your paper, then make a picture about it. Julie, you may draw anything you like today."

Julie looked up in surprise. She still had not said a word, but she was thinking! She knew what she would draw—Tabby!

The room was very still. Julie noticed that only one or two children started to work.

Mrs. King came and stood beside Julie. She laughed as she said, "Julie, some of us draw better than others. Some of us read very well. Some are good at math. We try to do our best no matter what we are doing. We play a game before we begin to draw a picture. See if you can tell what the boys and girls are doing."

Julie turned in her seat. The boys and girls had their eyes closed. Each one seemed to be thinking—HARD!

"Eyes open!" said Mrs. King, looking straight at Julie. She waited a minute. Then, turning to the boy beside Julie, she said, "Tell her about our game, Brad."

"We were trying to think how our picture is going to look when it is finished," said Brad. "I know about mine. May we begin?"

"You eager beavers may begin!" chuckled Mrs. King.

Crayolas and pencils came popping from the desks like magic. Julie watched the children. They were busy—and happy.

It was going to be hard to play deaf and dumb in Room 27.

4

Weekend Pets

There was that noise again! Julie closed her spelling book. She turned in the direction of the sound and peered over the heads of the boys and girls. In the back of the room there was a table. Was that a cage on it?

A soft voice behind Julie said, "You've finished, why don't you go take a look?"

Without thinking, Julie moved in the direction of the table. Was it what she thought it was? Yes! One—TWO of them!

Little whiskers twitched. Beady pink eyes looked up at Julie as if to say—and who are you? The big one raced around the cage and jumped into the wheel. Round and round it went, so fast you could hardly see it. He was putting on quite a show. As soon as the wheel slowed a bit, the smaller one jumped in, too. Julie almost laughed.

From behind her, the same kind voice said, "The big one is Mighty, the little one is Whitey. I think they like you."

A bell sounded in the hall. "Let's finish spelling," suggested Mrs. King. "We have lunch in five minutes."

Soon there were two neat rows lined up by the door— one of boys and one of girls. Everyone seemed to know just what to do—except Julie. She could feel the tears coming again, so she coughed to keep from crying.

Dana left the line and came to Julie. "I'm supposed to show you around the cafeteria. Mrs. King said I could. Do you have your money?" she asked.

Julie blindly felt inside her desk. There was her money—and a Kleenex.

Lunch was over. The afternoon passed quickly. Julie loved the story Mrs. King read to them, and the music period, but she was glad it was Friday.

"Almost time to go home," said Mrs. King. "Whose turn is it to take Mighty and Whitey for the weekend?" No one said a word.

Then Sam, with a surprised look on his face, said, "Mrs. King, may I look at the list? I think it's my turn."

"Yes, ma'am," said Sam, "it IS my turn, and we're going camping this weekend. Let me choose someone, please. Then maybe I can have that person's turn."

"A good idea, Sam," said Mrs. King. "Let's see who hasn't had a turn."

Julie held her breath! What if no one wanted Mighty and Whitey? Would they let a stranger take them? She wondered who Sam would choose. Then she saw it. Right there on her desk. It was the picture of Tabby.

Quickly Julie flipped the picture over. Her hand hit her spelling book. It landed on the floor with a bang! Everyone looked at Julie.

Sam said, "How about the new girl?"

"The new girl has a name, Sam. It's Julie. She would need to ask her Mother if it is convenient," said Mrs. King.

"But her mother is here," interrupted Dana, "I saw

her in the hall a minute ago. She has come for Julie
'cause it's her first day."

Mrs. King and Mrs. Grey had a talk outside the door.
Then the bell rang. In a few minutes Mighty, Whitey,
Julie, and Mrs. Grey were in the car. Mrs. King had
helped them carry the cage. She waved as the car started.
"See you Monday, Julie. Don't worry about your big
kitty. That is a safe cage for mice."

5

Flight 409

The days without Daddy were long. Every day Julie expected a letter. Saturday morning one arrived. As soon as Julie saw the writing, she began to run. At the kitchen door, she yelled, "Mother, it's a letter from Daddy!"

Mrs. Grey wiped her hands and ripped open the envelope. "Julie, Daddy says if we meet him at the airport in the morning, he will go to church with us!" said Mother.

"Daddy's coming! Daddy's coming!" Julie cried out. "Wake up, Tabby, you lazy cat, Daddy's coming!"

Poor Tabby. She never knew what to expect these days. Julie held her tight and danced around the kitchen. Then she raced upstairs to her bedroom. She dropped Tabby and picked up the binoculars.

How close and pretty the city looked through the glasses. Julie counted the steeples again—six of them! We are going to church—with Daddy—with Dad-dy! The words almost made a song!

The day finally passed—but Julie was too excited to go to sleep.

"Julie, it's morningtime," called Mother. Julie popped up like a jack-in-the-box. It couldn't be morning yet. She had just gone to sleep! The sun was shining through the bedroom window. Tabby stretched and jumped to the floor.

Julie was down the stairs before Mother poured her milk. She went straight to the utility room. She lifted the cover on the cage and said loudly, "Good morning, Mighty. Good morning, Whitey. Isn't it a nice day?" Both mice jumped into the wheel and raced round and round. "Stop, you sillies, and eat your breakfast," said Julie. "I'll play with you later."

Sometimes Julie was slow getting dressed. Not today.

"Julie, do you think you could open the garage door without getting dirty?" asked Mother.

"I think I can," said Julie. "Then I'll give Tabby some breakfast. She's chasing the birds again."

Mrs. Grey checked at the desk of the airport. Then she and Julie walked to Gate 3. Flight 409 was on time. The big plane seemed to glide out of the sky. One man signaled the pilot where to stop, another man rolled big steps up to the door. Julie was jumping up and down.

The plane door opened, and the first passenger appeared. Julie rushed through the big glass door, down the ramp, across the pavement to the foot of the steps.

"Daddy!" she screamed—and jumped into his arms.

The passengers coming down the steps smiled and carefully stepped over the crumpled clothes bag Mr. Grey had been carrying.

6

A Good-Night Talk

Mr. Grey sat on the side of the bed and rubbed Julie's back. "Been a good day?" he asked.

Julie sat up and hugged her Daddy until he groaned, "Ouch! Stop! Help! I'll have to call Mother!"

"No!" said Julie, turning loose quickly, "let's US just talk."

"Okay," said Mr. Grey, "let's talk. What's first?"

"When are you coming to Woodridge to stay—forever?" asked Julie.

"Can't say about forever, but I think I can be finished with my old job and be here in about two weeks," he said seriously. "That's not very long. Mother says that she and you—and Tabby—are getting adjusted."

"Maybe," said Julie thoughtfully, "but not Tabby!

She tries to catch the mockingbirds, and then they peck her on the head—every day."

"She'll learn, mockingbirds are new to her," Daddy explained.

"And she can't understand at all about Mighty and Whitey. I'm glad that is a good strong cage," Julie added.

"Do you keep them every weekend now?" asked Daddy.

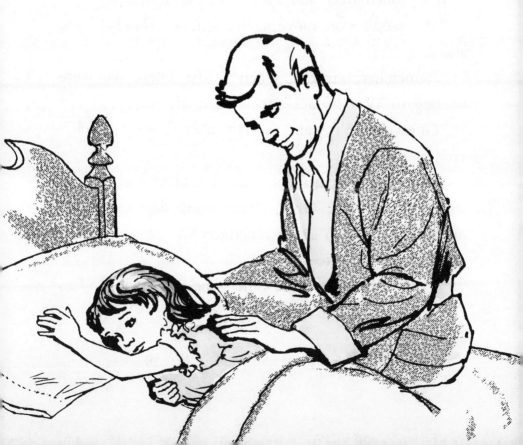

Julie grinned. "Well, Mrs. King saw how much I liked them the first day at school. Sam, then Dana, and then Janice let me have their turns."

"Think that might look a little selfish?" Daddy asked.

Julie sat up in bed and thought a minute. "Is it selfish when your friends GIVE you their turn?" She lay back on her pillow and added thoughtfully, "We're all friends in Room 27."

As Mr. Grey rubbed Julie's back again, he asked, "Want to talk about something else?"

Julie rolled over and looked at her father.

"We won't ever move again, will we Daddy?" she asked.

"Remember our talk when I first knew we were coming to Woodridge?" questioned Mr. Grey.

"Guess I don't want to remember it very much," confessed Julie.

"But you do remember what I told you about my job," insisted Mr. Grey, "that some day we might even have to go to another country?"

Julie was slow to reply.

"I think about it all the time," she admitted. "When

you are not here to rub my back, sometimes I can't go to sleep. I don't even have a sister to sleep in my room like Janice does."

"Mother and I have talked about that, Julie," said Daddy. "We're sorry, too, that you don't have a sister or brother. Have you thought any more about our adopting a baby?"

"Would you still love me? Would you have time to rub my back?" Julie asked.

Mother knocked on Julie's door, "Are you two going to talk all night?" she asked.

Mr. Grey tucked the covers in tight around Julie's shoulders. He gave her a good-night peck. Then he called, "I'm coming!"

To Julie he whispered, "If my plane didn't leave so early in the morning, I'd like to take you to school and meet Mrs. King. You get to know lots of nice people when you move."

7

Sick Inside

Daddy was gone. Julie felt all tight and funny inside. Her head hurt and her stomach ached. Maybe she had a fever!

Mother looked in the bedroom door. "Dressed yet?" she asked. "We need to leave for school in about ten minutes."

Julie sat on the side of the bed, still wearing her pajamas.

"Don't you feel like going to school today?" asked Mrs. Grey. She sat down and felt Julie's forehead.

"I think I'm sick—all inside," Julie answered. "I may have a fever."

"Well, we don't want to give Dana or Janice a 'catching' disease," Mother said. "Climb back under the covers, and I'll see if Dr. Jackson can see you this morning."

With that, she flipped out the light and went downstairs.

Julie lay very still. Dr. Jackson was Sam's father. She liked to go to his office, but what would he say?

"Julie," called Mother from downstairs, "I almost forgot. Daddy left a package for you on the dresser."

Julie jumped out of bed. She turned on the light and started to look for the package.

A small envelope marked JULIE was on the dresser. There was a box inside. On the snowy white cotton lay a tiny silver bell attached to a red leather collar. "This is not for me!" said Julie aloud. "It's for Tabby!" Then she saw the folded paper. The note said:

DEAR JULIE,

The red collar is for Tabby. Look under the cotton for your surprise. Wear it and remember that I love you.

DADDY

Julie lifted the cotton gently. There lay a ring with a green stone—her birthstone. She slipped it on her finger. It just matched the green dress she had picked out to wear today. Before she thought about being sick inside, she was dressed.

She hurried down the steps calling, "Tabby, here
kitty, kitty."

Mother tried not to look surprised. "You'll find
Tabby on the patio trying to catch a bird," she said.
"Going to give her some breakfast?"

"No, Daddy thinks she needs a bell to warn the
birds. Look! See what else was in the box. I can't wait
to show Dana."

"Tabby may not be very happy about that collar, Julie," explained Mother. "Why don't you wait until this afternoon to put it on her? Then you will be here to help her adjust to it. Breakfast is on the table, let's eat now."

Julie drank her juice. She was watching Tabby crouched under the bushes, waiting for a chance to catch a mockingbird. "She probably won't like that collar any better than she likes Mighty and Whitey," said Julie.

It was time to go. Julie opened the garage door. As Mrs. Grey passed the trash can, she tossed in a piece of paper she no longer needed. It read: Dr. Jackson ED 4-9651.

8

A Chance to Choose

Mrs. King worked at her desk. The boys and girls were enjoying their music period. Friday afternoon was a good time to have a few quiet minutes to think. She glanced at her plan book. This week had been full of surprises—the puppet show from Room 24, Sam's broken arm, and another new student yesterday.

Next week's plans were finished. Jane, Frank, and Sam would have a special interest in the new library book she would read each day. Brad and Frank would spark some enthusiasm for the weather film on Tuesday. The opening exercise on Thursday would help Sandi feel more like a part of the group.

Frank peeped around the door.

"Back so soon?" she asked in laughing tones.

"Yes, ma'am, we are!" Frank assured her. He was very proud of his job as line leader.

"And what report does the line leader have from Miss Blake?" the teacher asked.

"She said we were wonderful singers," Frank replied.

"Then you may come inside," said Mrs. King.

"Boys and girls," she said when they were settled in their seats, "I am always proud of you when other teachers tell me you are learning to work and play well together. Do you have a song to sing for me today?"

"We know all the words to 'America, the Beautiful,' " beamed Dana, "and Sandi knows it, too, even if she is from Australia."

"Fine," said Mrs. King. Looking at Dana, she asked, "Did Miss Blake decide which boys and girls will sing for opening exercise next Thursday?"

Without a trace of a smile, Dana said, "No ma'am." Then beaming all over she added, "She let us choose."

"Then let's practice our program," said Mrs. King. "Sam, take your place by the desk to lead the Pledge of Allegiance. Those chosen to sing will stand by the windows. The rest of us will be good listeners."

The practice was over. It was almost time for the bell.

"Whose turn to take Mighty and Whitey this weekend?" Mrs. King asked the class.

Julie remembered what Daddy had said. She couldn't take them again. She raised her hand.

"Mrs. King," she said, "may I talk to you—at your desk—a minute?"

40

Mrs. King nodded.

"Remember when Sam let me have his turn?" she whispered. "Well, since he has a broken arm and can't play outside much, maybe he could take them today."

Mrs. King smiled.

"Sam," she called, "will you come to the desk, please?" She spoke softly, "Julie thinks you might like to take Mighty and Whitey today, would you?"

"Yes, ma'am," said Sam. Then he paused. "That cage is pretty heavy to carry with one hand. Maybe the new girl would take them."

"Oh, Mrs. King, ask her, please," exclaimed Julie. "I saw her watching them. It might help her—to—adjust!"

"You think so?" asked Mrs. King. "Sandi, will you come to the desk?"

Julie was late getting to the car.

"All by yourself?" asked Mother, "and this is Friday?"

"Oh, I've had turns with Mighty and Whitey," said Julie. "Sandi Kemp, the new girl from Australia, who lives just down the hill, is taking them today. That's why I was late. I was telling her how to take care of them. Maybe I'll go to her house tomorrow to see them."

41

9

The Escape

The doorbell rang! Julie was getting dressed to go to the public library. On Saturday morning Mrs. Carroll told good stories. There were lots of book to check out.

From upstairs Julie heard Mother say, "Oh, you must be Sandi! Are you having trouble with Mighty and Whitey?"

Julie came down the steps two at a time.

"Sandi," she cried, "What's the matter? Are Mighty and Whitey sick?"

Julie's new friend was trying hard to hold back the tears. Julie looked at the covered cage, the can of food, and the thin sweater Sandi was wearing. The cool, crisp air rushed in the front door.

"Do come inside, Sandi," said Mrs. Grey. "I'll get you girls some hot chocolate." She started to the kitchen.

That sad, troubled face caused her to turn and ask, "your mother knows where you are, doesn't she, Sandi?"

At this question Sandi burst into tears and shook her head from side to side. Mrs. Grey sat down on the footstool and put an arm around Sandi.

"Julie, please take Mighty and Whitey to the utility room and see that they are warm. We'll have some chocolate after I call Sandi's mother. Maybe Sandi can go to the library with us!"

In the bright, cheerful kitchen, Julie and Sandi sat on high stools in front of the counter. Small curls of steam came from the mugs.

Mother wiped the cabinet tops and asked, "Sandi, do you have brothers and sisters?"

In her clipped British accent, Sandi answered, "Yes, ma'am, one bigger and one smaller."

At the mention of "one bigger" her face again clouded. She explained, "Big sisters are afraid of mice, even in a cage. But if one gets loose in the house—"

"You mean you let Mighty and Whitey out of the cage?" asked Julie.

"Not on purpose," continued Sandi. "You see, in

this new house, I have to share a room with my big sister. She doesn't like anything!"

All was quiet for a moment. Then Sandi continued, "I was lonesome, so I hid the cage behind my bed. I just wanted to feel their soft little fur."

"So—" Julie said.

"Betty came into the room. When she screamed, I

dropped Mighty! He ran right under her. It was frightful! All the screaming woke up Danny. Then Daddy came to catch Mighty and missed the news. Nothing goes right here!" she said sadly.

Mother glanced at Julie. "If you girls will excuse me, I'll get dressed. We need to stop by Sandi's house for her coat on the way to the library."

As Mother went up the stairs, Tabby came down.

"If it's very soft fur you like, Sandi, why don't you pet Tabby?" Julie asked. Tabby rubbed the chair leg, then jumped into Julie's lap.

Sandi just stared out the window. A mockingbird was picking orange berries from a brightly colored bush.

"Things are different here," Sandi said almost in a whisper. "Even the birds! I wish I could go home—to Australia."

At that moment Mrs. Grey appeared. The two girls joined her for an interesting Saturday morning trip to the library. Sandi liked Mrs. Carroll's stories as much as Julie did. Then each girl chose two books to check out of the big public library.

Mrs. Grey and Julie took Sandi home before turning in their own driveway.

45

Tabby lay on the lounge chair in the sunshine. She stretched and yawned as Julie hopped out of the car and went to sit beside her. Tabby spotted the sash of Julie's dress. She rolled on her back and caught it with all four feet.

Julie picked Tabby up and held her close. The little silver bell on the red leather collar make a tinkling sound. Tabby hit at it with her paw and looked into Julie's eyes.

Julie stroked Tabby's sleek fur. "Tabby," she sighed, "I know you don't like this collar. But the mockingbirds don't like your catching their babies either."

Julie was thoughtful. Tabby's purr grew louder as Julie stroked her back.

"Tabby," she said slowly, "changes are hard for all of us—including Sandi—but we can adjust happily."